# Lullaby &

# Good Night

## SONGS FOR SWEET DREAMS

### ILLUSTRATED BY

## JULIE DOWNING

SIMON & SCHUSTER BOOKS FOR YOUNG READERS

*Lullabies are loved* by both
parents and children alike. I remember
the feeling of comfort and safety when my
mother sang to me. After my own children were born,
I wanted to share some favorite lullabies with them.

Falling asleep can be difficult for young children, and a lullaby
soothes the transition between bedtime and sleep. This book is a
collection of some traditional lullabies and some less familiar songs.
I chose them for their poetic quality as well as the way they illustrate
the transition between evening and dreaming. A melody line is provided
in the borders to give the reader the essence of the song, but the lullabies
can be read or sung to a different tune. Most important is taking time to
share a precious moment together.

*Sweet dreams!*                                                    —JULIE DOWNING

# Contents

## Golden Slumbers

### TRADITIONAL ENGLISH

Golden slumbers kiss your eyes
Smiles awake you when you rise
Sleep, pretty baby, do not cry
And I will sing a lullaby.

# Starlight, Starbright

**TRADITIONAL**

Starlight, Starbright
First star I see tonight,
Wish I may, wish I might
Have the wish I wish tonight.

## Now the Day Is Over

WORDS BY SABINE BARING-GOULD

Now the day is over,
Night is drawing nigh;
Shadows of the evening
Steal across the sky.

Now the darkness gathers,
Stars begin to peep;
Birds and beasts and flowers
Soon will be asleep.

Father, give the weary
Calm and sweet repose;
With thy tender blessing,
May our eyelids close.

Through the long night watches
May thine angels spread
Their white wings above me,
Watching around my bed.

## Hush, Little Baby

### TRADITIONAL ENGLISH

Hush, little baby, don't say a word,
Papa's gonna buy you a mockingbird.
And if that mockingbird won't sing,
Papa's gonna buy you a diamond ring.
If that diamond ring turns brass,
Papa's gonna buy you a looking glass.
If that looking glass gets broke,
Papa's gonna buy you a billy goat.
If that billy goat won't pull,
Papa's gonna buy you a cart and bull.
If that cart and bull turn over,
Papa's gonna buy you a dog named Rover.
If that dog named Rover won't bark,
Papa's gonna buy you a horse and cart.
If that horse and cart fall down,
You'll be the sweetest little baby in town.

## I See the Moon

**TRADITIONAL IRISH**

I see the moon and the moon sees me,
The moon sees the somebody I want to see.
God bless the moon and God bless me,
And God bless the somebody I want to see.

It seems as though the Lord above,
Created you for me to love.
He picked you out from all the rest,
Because he knew I'd love you the best.

## Kumbaya

### BLACK SPIRITUAL

Kumbaya, my Lord,
Kumbaya.
Kumbaya, my Lord,
Kumbaya.
Kumbaya, my Lord,
Kumbaya.
Oh Lord, Kumbaya.

Someone's cryin', my Lord,
Kumbaya.
Someone's cryin', my Lord,
Kumbaya.
Someone's cryin', my Lord,
Kumbaya.
Oh Lord, Kumbaya.

Someone's singin', my Lord,
Kumbaya . . .

Someone's laughin', my Lord,
Kumbaya . . .

Someone's sleepin', my Lord,
Kumbaya . . .

Someone's dreamin', my Lord,
Kumbaya . . .

## El Coquí (The Tree Frog)

**PUERTO RICAN**

El coquí, el coquí a mi me encanta,
Es tan lindo el cantar del coquí;
Por las noches al ir a acostarme, me adormece cantando asi:
Co-quí! Co-quí! Co-quí-quí-quí-quí!
Co-quí! Co-quí! Co-quí-quí-quí-quí!

*English:*

Coquí, coquí, I love the coquí,
He sings a lovely song;
Each night in my sleep he calls to me:
Co-kee! Co-kee! Co-kee-kee-kee-kee!
Co-kee! Co-kee! Co-kee-kee-kee-kee!

## All the Pretty Little Horses
### TRADITIONAL AMERICAN SOUTH

Hush-a-bye, don't you cry,
Go to sleepy little baby.
When you wake, you shall have
All the pretty little horses.
Blacks and bays, dapples and grays,
Coach and six little horses.

All the pretty little horses.

## Wynken, Blynken and Nod

**WORDS BY EUGENE FIELD**

**BASED ON A TRADITIONAL DUTCH LULLABY**

Wynken, Blynken and Nod one night
Sailed off in a wooden shoe—
Sailed on a river of crystal light,
Into a sea of dew.
"Where are you going and what do you wish?"
The old moon asked the three.
"We have come to fish for the herring fish
That swim in the beautiful sea;
Nets of silver and gold have we,"
Said Wynken, Blynken and Nod.

The old moon laughed and sang a song
As they rocked on the wooden shoe.
And the wind that sped them all night long
Ruffled the waves of dew.
The little stars were the herring fish
That lived in the beautiful sea.
"Now cast your nets wherever you wish,
Never afeared are we!"
So cried the stars to the fishermen three,
Wynken, Blynken and Nod.

All night long their nets they threw
To the stars in the twinkling foam.
Then down from the skies came the wooden shoe,
Bringing the fishermen home.
'Twas all so pretty a sail it seemed,
As if it could not be,
And some folks thought 'twas a dream they dreamed
Of sailing that beautiful sea.
But I shall name you the fishermen three,
Wynken, Blynken and Nod.

Wynken and Blynken are two little eyes,
And Nod a little head.
And the wooden shoe that sailed the skies
Is a wee one's trundle bed.
So shut your eyes while Mother sings
Of wonderful sights that be,
And you shall see the beautiful things
As you rock in the misty sea.
Where the old shoe rocked the fishermen three,
Wynken, Blynken and Nod.

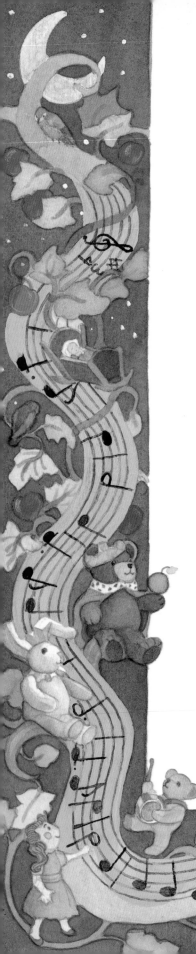

## *Rock-a-bye Baby*

### TRADITIONAL ENGLISH

Rock-a-bye baby, on the tree top,
When the wind blows, the cradle will rock.
When the bough breaks, the cradle will fall,
And down will come baby, cradle and all.

Rock-a-bye baby, your cradle is green,
Father's a king, and mother's a queen.
Sister's a lady and wears a gold ring, and
Brother's a drummer and plays for the king.

Rock-a-bye baby, way up on high,
Never mind baby, mother is nigh.
Up to the ceiling, down to the ground,
Rock-a-bye baby, up hill and down.

## Twinkle, Twinkle

WORDS BY JANE TAYLOR

Twinkle, twinkle, little star,
How I wonder what you are!
Up above the world so high,
Like a diamond in the sky.
Twinkle, twinkle, little star,
How I wonder what you are!

When the blazing sun is gone,
When he nothing shines upon.
Then you show your little light,
Twinkle, twinkle, all the night.
Twinkle, twinkle, little star,
How I wonder what you are!

Then the traveler in the dark
Thanks you for your tiny spark!
He could not see which way to go
If you did not twinkle so.
Twinkle, twinkle, little star,
How I wonder what you are!

In the dark blue sky you keep,
Often through my curtains peep.
For you never shut your eye,
Till the sun is in the sky.
Twinkle, twinkle, little star,
How I wonder what you are!

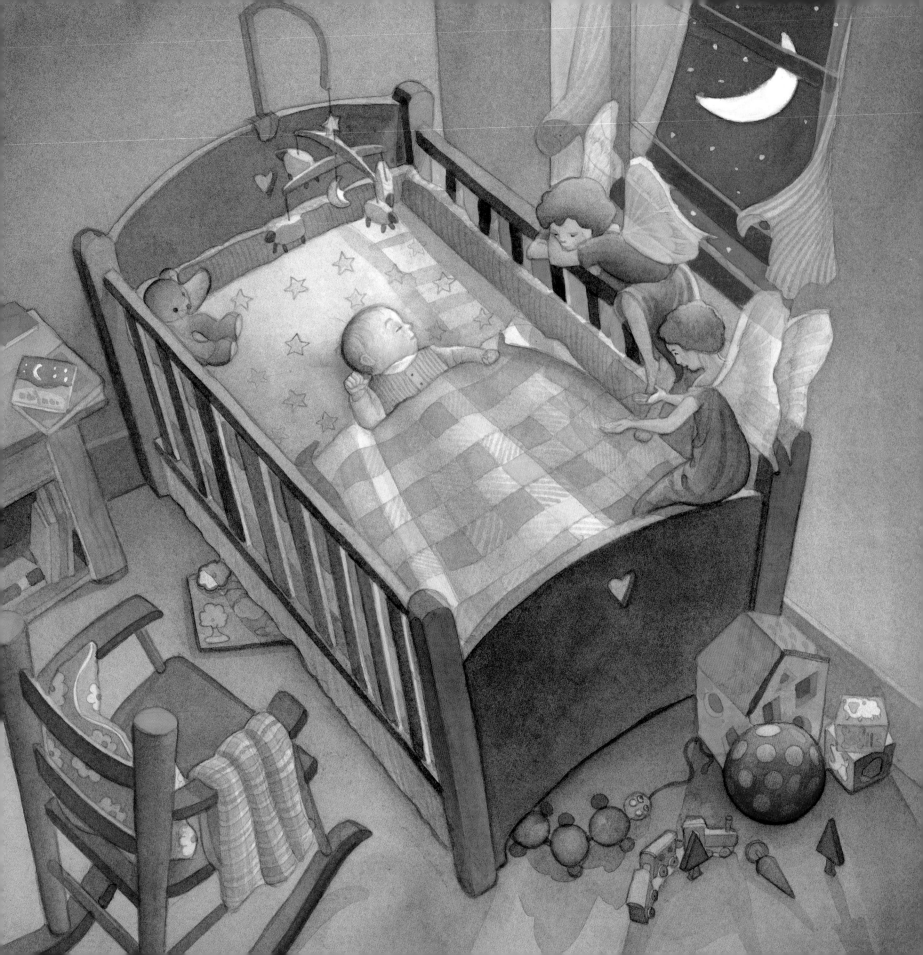

## All Through the Night

TRADITIONAL WELSH

Sleep my child and peace attend thee,
All through the night;
Guardian angels God will send thee,
All through the night;
Soft the drowsy hours are creeping,
Hill and vale in slumber sleeping,
I, my loving vigil keeping,
All through the night.

While the moon her watch is keeping,
All through the night;
While the weary world is sleeping,
All through the night;
O'er thy spirit gently stealing,
Visions of delight revealing,
Breathes a pure and holy feeling,
All through the night.

## Baby's Boat

**THOMAS DECKER**

Baby's boat's a silver moon
Sailing in the sky,
Sailing o'er a sea of sleep
While the stars float by.

*Chorus*
    Sail, baby, sail
    Out upon the sea;
    Only don't forget to sail
    Back again to me.

Baby's fishing for a dream,
Fishing far and near.
Her line a silver moonbeam is,
Her bait a silver star.

*Repeat Chorus*

## Lullaby and Good Night

**TRADITIONAL**

Lullaby and good night,
Sleep is softly around you.
While your dreams fill your eyes
With a melody of love,
Close your eyes now and rest,
May your slumbers be blessed.
Go to sleep now and rest,
May these hours be blessed.

## To William Charles
### with thanks to Madeline, Belden, Kai, Aaron, Andrea, and Oscar

## Simon & Schuster Books for Young Readers

An imprint of Simon & Schuster Children's Publishing Division
1230 Avenue of the Americas, New York, New York 10020

Compilation and illustrations copyright © 1999 by Julie Downing
All rights reserved including the right of reproduction in whole or in part in any form.
SIMON & SCHUSTER BOOKS FOR YOUNG READERS is a trademark of Simon & Schuster.
Transcriptions by Sandy Cressman
Original music for "Now the Day Is Over" by J. Barnaby
Original music for "Twinkle, Twinkle" by Wolfgang Mozart
Original music for "Lullaby and Good Night" by Johannes Brahms
Design by Heather Wood / The text for this book is set in Fairfield Medium.
The illustrations are rendered in watercolor. Printed in Hong Kong
1    3    5    7    9    10    8    6    4    2

Library of Congress Cataloging-in-Publication Data
Lullaby and good night : songs for sweet dreams /
collected and illustrated by Julie Downing.
p.  cm.
Summary : An illustrated collection of classic lullabies.
ISBN 0-689-81085-7
1. Children's poetry. 2. Lullabies. [1. Lullabies.] I. Downing, Julie.
PN6110.C4L86    1999    782.4215'82'0268—dc21    97-47306